T0197568

To order additional copies of this book, contact:
Xlibris
844-714-8691
www.Xlibris.com
Orders@Xlibris.com

ISBN: Softcover   978-1-4535-9100-0
        EBook   978-1-6698-4103-6

Print information available on the last page

Rev. date: 07/29/2022

We wake to the fresh smell of coffee, and cinnamon toast. And the voices of Grandma and Grandpa. By time we awake, they are dressed and ready to start the day. We all say good morning. And ask Grandma or Grandpa what the weather was going to be like out side for the day, so we would know how to dress for our chores. For instance, if it is going to rain we would need to wear rubber boots. Also a raincoat and a hat. Or if it was going to be cold, we would want to dress in warm cloths. If it is going to be nice out, we would just wear old jeans and a tee shirt. Boots are the safest type of foot wear. Or tennis shoes, but sandals were not safe at all for the type of work we had to do. So we would get a quick bite to eat, and something to drink. Just something to hold us over until we got the chores done. Because when the chores were all done Grandma and Lonna would have us a good breakfast cooked up. Which was always something that would at least stick to your ribs. We have several animals to take care of. So we have a lot of responsibility to our farm animals, to make sure the animals are well taken care of. This is very important to maintain healthy animals. Which keeps them happy. The animals look forward to the care they get from us every day. They love to get attention. Our Grandma and Grandpa live with us. They are very helpful with the chores we all share. We enjoy their company, and they enjoy ours. They tell us lots of interesting stories. We are very fortunate to have them live with us. We enjoy spending time with our family, friends and neighbors. We usually are outside in the fresh country air. Weather permitting. The garden is the last chore of the day. This can be done in the evening before or after supper. The Garden is very special, because we call it our community garden. Even our neighbors come to our farm and offer to help with it. We make sure we share all of our food we get from the garden. Every one gets to enjoy the fresh vegetables we all grow in it.

Let us talk a little about the chores we do around the farm. Jeff and his Dad take care of the horses. The horses are so pretty. We have fun just watching them. We go horse back riding about four to five times a week. Riding the horses is so much fun! And it gives the horses the exercise they need. It is very important for them to get their exercise. Keeps them healthy and happy! After we are done riding them we take off their saddle and the rest of their gear. Then we wash them down with soap and water. Then we rinse them off with the water hose.

When they are dry we brush them down to make them look good . Plus this will help them get rid of any loose hair. The horses love all the attention. Horses also need their hoofs picked clean with a special tool. Their hoofs are their feet. The special tool to clean their hoofs, is called a hoof pick. This is a dangerous job! It is best to hire some one to do this for you. This person is called a Farrier. It is kind of expensive, but it is worth it! Jeff and his Dad feed the horses cracked corn and hay. Sometimes we give them sweet feed. They get this after we ride them for being so good to us .And letting us enjoy, a nice fun time riding them. In the summer it is hotter so we give them fresh water twice a day. Some times the horses will show off and make funny faces. They turn their top lip up and it looks like they are smiling. Or they will lay on their backs and roll back and forth on their backs. This is a good way for them to itch their backs. We have two girl horses and two boy horses. The girl horse's names are Windy Sue and Ginger Snaps. The two boy horse's names are Smokey and spot. All of the horses are very pretty. We have a big barn where they love to lay in and sleep. Also that is where they get fed their hay and corn. Plus it a place where they can get out of the hot sun. The barn also protects them from the weather. The horses love to go out into the green fields to eat grass, soaking up the sun. Our horses are lots of fun! One time Steve and Lonna went for a horse ride. They took their son Jeff with them. Jeff was only three years old. Jeff road with his Mom, Lonna. Steve and Lonna are husband and wife. With one son, Jeff. Windy Sue is the horse Lonna and Jeff were riding. Steve road Spot. They were riding on a trail they usually took, when on their close to home ride. It was in the woods way back in there behind the Lake. It had been raining the day before really hard. So there was a lot of water everywhere. Even on the trails. There is a creek that runs threw the woods; and this water goes into the Lake. You have to cross the creek, to get to the trail on the other side of the creek. This is the trail that they always took. But that one day, the creek was up very high because of the rain from the day before. So Steve went first. He made it. But Lonna and little three year old Jeff, road Windy Sue to close to Steve who was riding Spot. Spot and Steve had to go slower than Lonna was expecting, and she had to stop. When she stopped, Windy began to sink in the creek. Lonna tried to get Windy to follow Spot, but she could not move. Windy was already sinking too much. Windy began to panic! This scared Lonna! She was scared for Jeff and the horse. Steve saw they were in serious trouble. He jumped off of Spot really quick! And ran over to the edge of the creek to help. The creek had steep sides. Lonna tried to stay calm for Jeff's sake and for Windys. But Windy was still sinking! Windy was already almost to her belly. Lonna knew she had to get Jeff to safety and quick! Steve could see this too! So Lonna took Jeff by his arm and told him I am gonna swing you over to your daddy. He will catch you. Lonna Swung Jeff with one really good hard swing. He went flying in the air, almost four to five feet in the air! Steve caught Jeff! And got him to a safe spot. Until Lonna could get there. Well Lonna knew she had to get to her son Jeff. Which would also take some weight off of Windy. So, Lonna got off the horse grabbed the reins and pulled at them while still in the cold muddy water. Windy Sue tried to move but could not. She had sunk too much! Now the water was just about to the top of Windys back. Lonna had to get herself out of the creek before she sank too. Or the horse could roll over on her and pin her under, Windy. Which, would have probably drowned Lonna. Steve told Lonna, get out of there and come take care of Jeff. So she got out of the creek and got to her son! She held Jeff real tight and started to cry. Then Jeff got scared and began to cry too. Steve got back in the creek to try and help Windy, before she sank so bad she would drown for sure. She was almost completely covered in water. Only top of her back and rear end, and neck and head was still above water. Steve found a tree limb, and he did not want to hurt her, but it was all he could do to maybe get her out. He swatted her in the rear end while Lonna pulled the reins calling her to please Windy come here. Come on girl, come on!! It did not work. The Horse was in shock! Poor thing, she was so scared, us too! But the Horse was sinking to her death. If we could not get her out, she would die right there. Nothing would work. So now she had sank more from trying to get out. Only her nose and mouth were visible now. Steve told Lonna, to go as fast as she could and get help! While he stayed there and gave the horse the comfort of him being there. We loved her so much! We had her since she was a baby. He would also make sure that he did his best to keep her nose and mouth above water. That was all you could see, it was sad; and horrible. Lonna was holding Onto Jeff tight, and took off through the woods for home. Lonna saw two 4wheelers out there riding around. And she started screaming for them to, HELP! HELP! Thankfully they saw her; and road over to Lonna quick! They knew something was wrong. Lonna told the two men what had happened and asked them to please go help my husband! So the two 4wheelers went in the direction Lonna told them. Mean while Lonna was still holding Jeff tight against her while she kept running for home. Now Lonna was in shock! Little Jeff probably was too. Lonna was not sure what she would do when she got home, but she kept on running! She was worried about her husband and Windy Sue! While running home Lonna thought of a good idea. To call a very close friend of theirs, John. He had a 4wheel drive truck, with a comalong. She knew his truck could pull Windy out. If only he would be home and answer his phone. So, when she got to the farm home she took care of Jeff first. Put a blanket on him and gave him a sippy cup of water. Then she gave John a call. Thank goodness he answered! Lonna told him what was happening. And he said he would be right there! He lived 15 miles away, but he must have drove like the wind. He is one of our favorite horse back riders to ride with! So Lonna Waited there for him. That way she could explain where Steve was. Mean while, the two men she saw on the 4wheeler bikes, had found Steve and Windy Sue! Steve was very cold and scared and so was Windy! The two men had a comalong on their 4wheelers and they tried and tried to pull Windy out! With Steve Pushing on her rear end. And calling to her! They were all trying as hard as they could to get Windy out of the muddy creek. Finally John pulled up. He got out of his truck as fast as he could! Ran over to Lonna, and she told him right where Steve and Windy was. John Knew exactly where they were. And he got ready to go back behind the woods, when all of the sudden; Steve and Windy Sue came walking up slowly!! We were so happy to see them! Lonna could not believe it. John was so Happy too, seeing them walking up! Steve was walking her, because she was in so much shock! Steve told Lonna to go inside and grab all the dry towels and blankets she could find! Quick he said, hurry! Steve and John started to wrap Windy Sue in the blankets first. When she quit shaking Steve and John started to dry her off with the clean dry towels. Lonna gave Steve a coat to put on him self. For he was so cold and shaking too. Steve told Lonna To go into the house and call our neighbor, Rick. To tell him what has happened, and to please come here and bring some medicine for Windy, to keep her from getting sick with pneumonia or with any other kind of sickness. Plus we told him she was in shock, but getting better on her shaking. So Rick came right over with three different kinds of shots for Windy. He is really good with helping out sick animals. Rick only lived one mile away so he was there very quick! Very good to help out your neighbors, because some day they may need our help and we would be right there too. And John bless his heart, as far away as he lived; he was there so fast! We are grateful, to every one who helped us! We do not even know, the two men who helped pull Windy out of the creek.

Thank goodness Lonna saw them in the woods as she was running back to the farm. While carrying Jeff in her arms. This was quit a remarkable thing. Getting all the help we did. Lonna and Jeff were just fine. Steve was to after he got out of his muddy wet, cold cloths. Took a shower and put on clean dry cloths. And we are so thankful , that Windy Sue pulled through it real well. Except she was scared of any water out riding from then on. She was scared to go through a water puddle, so she would jump it. So you just had to be hanging on or the jump might through a person off. Lonna was still crying a little because she felt like it was all her fault, for following to close behind another rider. This is true, Lonna did ride to close behind. But Lonna will never do that again!! Steve thanked her for her fast running through the woods. And everything she did. Especially, Considering Lonna was carrying Jeff. And in shock herself. So a lesson for us all to learn, do not follow to close to another rider when horse back riding!! Things were back to normal for Windy in about four to five days. Except for Windy was always afraid of riding threw any water holes, puddles or any thing that had to do with water. Hopefully this terrible experience, has taught someone else a lesson besides Lonna!

We also have one Rooster, and five chickens. They live in a big pen which is connected to the out side of the big barn . This is the chickens home where they live, once they are big enough too. There are little boxes made from wood. This is where they sleep, and lay their big brown eggs. Their pen protects them from the weather and predators. Predators such as Mink, Skunks, foxes, and any mean dogs that may come to our farm. All the girl chickens, we just call them girl friends. The Roosters name is Lucky. The girl chickens lay us eggs every day. The Eggs are big and brown color. The eggs taste very good! So fresh. The Rooster will try and protect the girl chickens. The girl chickens are called Hens. Or some times we call them egg layers. Lonna loves the chickens the best. Roosters can be very mean! Roosters have spurs on their legs. Just above their feet. Spurs are razor sharp. They can hurt you very bad! One time when Lonna was a little girl 3 years old, her Grandmas favorite rooster spurred Lonna real bad! It spurred her all over the back of her neck and head. The blood was coming out so quick, it covered her whole face. Grandma, and Lonna's Mom did not know where that mean old Rooster had spurred her; for there was to much blood. Lonna Was crying a lot! She was in pain! And the blood was burning her eyes! They grabbed Lonna, and took her to the Hospital. They put a few stitches in the back of her neck, and a few in a couple spots on her head. When they got back From the Hospital, Lonna's Mom put her to bed so she could rest. Then Grandma went out side and rung that mean old Roosters neck. And then she buried it. This was Grandmas pet, but the thing just got really mean! And after what it did to Lonna, she knew she had to get rid of it. This made Grandma cry, only because she really did love that old rooster. And it made her so mad at What he had done to little Lonna. This should teach every one a lesson about roosters, they can be very dangerous to people and dogs or cats. Here at the farm, now that Lonna is older; and married to Steve and they have a son Jeff. Now Grandma and Grandpa live with Lonna and her family. But Lonna and her Grandma, take care of the chickens; and the rooster. They feed and water them every day.

They also gather the nice big brown eggs every day. Chickens get very messy, so their water and feed containers get a rinse off every day. The eggs have to be cleaned when brought into the house, before they go in the ice box. You can enjoy these eggs, in many different ways! In cake recipes, pies, fried up with your breakfast, or just boil them to eat. They are so tasty! We buy baby chicks every year. They will be ready to start laying eggs at about five to six months old. We order our baby chicks from a special magazine. The company we order from will mail them to the Post Office. The Post Office will call, us as soon as they arrive there. We will go to the Post Office to pick them up. And take them home to the farm. This will be their new home for the rest of their lives. They will get their first drink of water and eat their first bite of food, when they get to their new little home. I say little homes, because when they are young baby chicks; they have to stay in a small pen. Where we keep a heat light on them to keep them warm. When they get big enough, they will go out side with the older chickens, in the big pen. Where there, they will become egg layers like the rest of the older chickens. They will learn a lot from the big chickens. Like to go inside the little boxes to sleep, and some day lay their eggs in them. The oldest chicken we ever had, lived to be seven years old. So that is why we buy new baby chicks every year. So we will always have egg layers. The chickens are a lot of fun for the kids to visit with. Because the Kids love to feed them grass, or bread through the little holes in the fence that protects the chickens, and keeps them protected from other predators. Chickens will eat almost any thing. They love to eat bugs, or left over vegetables from the dinner table. Once Lonna saw a mouse in the chicken pen, it could not get out. It did not take the chickens long before they had that poor little mouse ate.

Sometimes a bird will fly into the chicken's pen, when we have the door open to water and feed them. Grandma and Lonna will help the little bird fly out. The chickens can not catch a bird any way. So at least they can not eat the little bird. Sometimes when Jeff is feeding the chickens blades of grass, the chickens will peck at his fingers and bite him. Jeff will just smile because it does not hurt. It only startles him! He just keeps right on feeding them. Kids do love the chickens, they like to feed them and they know they could get bit too. But I think they think it is funny. The chickens and rooster are so pretty. We raise Road Island Reds and also black and white stripped Dominecors. The only time we notice them to stink is after a lot of rain. Every year our two neighbor kids, barrow a couple of our chickens to take to 4H club. FFA is a class at your school; most schools have this class to take. FFA Stands for Future Farmers of America. 4H will come to schools who have FFA and try and get people who are interested in this field. To join up with 4H. This is where you can show animals, and win awards. Sometimes even money. It is a very fun and rewarding class to take. Teaches you a lot about all kinds of animals. And about planting different kinds of things. Like Trees, grass, Gardens. Our chickens always have won a ribbon for being so well taken care of. This shows, by how healthy they look and how pretty they are. This makes the neighbor kids happy! And it makes us proud of our chickens. Shows how well we take care of them, which makes us feel like all the work we do with them, is really putting out some healthy chickens.

Lonna was raised in the city, Jeff was born and raised in the country. So was Jeff's Dad, born in the country and raised in the country. Our Grandparents were born in the country and lived there all of their lives. We are so glad to be able to share our every day lives together. We love every thing we do on the farm together. Each of us helping out with every thing around the farm. We love, having our Grandparents with us teaching us so much; each and every day. They also teach us a lot about how to have a good Garden. When Steve works at his job, the rest of us have more to do. We just help out where ever we can. When Steve gets back from work, he pitches in and helps us with somethings, only he can do the best at.

On our Farm we also have Cows too. We only have enough land to raise seven cows at one time. Rule of thumb is one cow to one acre of land. We let our cows and Horses have ten acres to live on. The other ten acres, we grow our own hay on. We will use this hay to feed our animals. There is usually enough to last the animals, to feed them; from one year to next. This saves us a lot of money. We buy our whole kernel corn from the feed store. The feed store is what you call a store where you buy animal food from. And many other things, like pet supplies. Plants for the Garden.

They also sale dog food, cat food, fish food, about any kind of animal food you can think of. Also the people there are so nice. They are very helpful too, with any questions you may have. We buy the whole kernel corn there because it is much cheaper. When we get home we put the corn in a special farm machine, called a hammer mill. It grinds the corn. Which we grind it to cracked corn pieces. It last longer, it is easier for the animals to eat and digest.

We buy our baby calves when they are just a few days old. So they are so small, we have to feed them by using a very big baby bottle. This is a special bottle that you can buy from the feed store. We use what is called milk replacer. It is full of vitamins and lots of good healthy things in it. Just like what the mother cow would have in her milk. The baby calves are called, bull calves. Until we band them, which this turns them into a steer. That is the way we do most of our young calves. If we want any of our cows to get pregnant, we put them in with our neighbors Bull. This may take a couple months. Then we bring our pregnant cows back to the farm. They take about nine months to be ready to give birth. We do this with the two, cows we have. We keep them just for having young baby calves. Soon as they are old enough to get them off the milk replacer, we let them start drinking water from a water trough. A lot of farmers use old cast iron bath tubs for the trough. Or you can buy one from the feed store. When they get a little bigger, we put them out in the pasture, with the other bigger cows and steers. They all get along just fine. The cows get attached to them, and they will protect them from about any thing. Some of the cattle's predators are coyote's, a pack of wild dogs, and hunters . They cannot see camouflage very well, and this bothers them. So they will run a hunter off their field. The calves will learn from the bigger cattle how to eat the grass in the fields. They all get along just fine. The animal Doctor is called, a Veterinarian. He makes sure the cattle and the horses stay healthy. He gives them Shots once a year to keep them from getting sick. Veterinarians are very nice people and they love all animals. As the cattle get bigger you should be very careful around them. They kick a lot, and could accidently kick you! This could hurt you very bad. Are Horses and cattle are kept in the same field, they get along just fine. We have an electric fence around the field, to keep them in their field. If they touch this it will shock them, which will teach them to stay in the field. This shock hurts them a little, enough so they will not do it again.

Sometimes deers will run through the fence to get to where they want to go. This unfortunately will break the fence. Then we all get together and go out and fix and repair the fence.

After a bad storm the old trees will sometimes fall on the fence and break it. So again we all get together, go to the place where the broken tree is on the fence. Then it takes a strong man to use a chain saw, and cut the tree into smaller pieces. So it can be moved and we can fix the fence. Then we pick up the cut up pieces of wood, from the broken tree and take it back to the farm, and put it on a pile. This will be the wood we use for our camp fires. Working together is a good way to keep things done. If some one was to get hurt or just need some help, we could count on some one being there to help out! We do get a lot of fire wood from keeping the fence clear, or from old trees dropping branches down in our yard. We all like to have camp fires, and cook hot dogs over it. Or cook marshmallows. Or just sit by it and enjoy talking to each other. Telling stories, is always fun too. It is relaxing to just sit by a camp fire, plus if it is cool out; it is a good way to warm up. And if you wanted to fish at night it helps give off light.

We have one Dog. His name is Joe. He is very smart. He knows how to shake hands, sit, stay, fetch, and he minds us well. When we go hunting Joe always wants to come with us. So we have to put him on a chain, or put him in the house. If he goes in the house, Grandma or Grandpa will watch him. They like to have him in, rather than on a chain. If he was to follow us it would ruin our hunting. We do let him follow us when we go horse back riding. He is also a good watch dog! Steve taught Lonna how to hunt when she was about fifteen years old. Taught her how to be safe!! Steve bought Lonna a single shot, twenty gauge shot gun. They were out in the woods hunting for squirrels one early morning. Steve told Lonna where to go in the woods, and just move slowly. Squirrels have very good eyes, so you have to move very slowly! Steve told Lonna, when you see a squirrel find a place where you can sit down. Or to lean against a tree. He said to wait for a good shot at it. Steve told her to think before you shoot. Make sure of the direction you are shooting, is safe for any neighbors living any where that way. And be careful if shooting his way. It is always safest, when you shoot up into the trees. And always keep the safety on. Until you are sure you have a good safe shot. Steve always try's to stay about one city block away from Lonna. Just in case there ever was an accident. Well they split up and they went their own ways. Steve always knowing where Lonna was. He is a VERY GOOD SAFE hunter. Lonna saw her first squirrel! It is always exciting, she made sure of the shot; and then she pulled the trigger.

She got it! But what she did not know, is that the squirrel was only wounded. It stood up on its back legs and was looking for who had just hurt him. Well Lonna stood up to go over to the squirrel and pick it up, to go into her pouch on her vest she was wearing. The wounded squirrel saw her! It was hurt and mad! It went straight for her! Since the gun Lonna was using was a single shot she had to hurry and reload it. When she went to open the gun, it opened up real wide. The gun just fell apart into two pieces..Meanwhile the wounded squirrel, was still coming straight for her! Lonna could not get the gun to go back together. So she screamed for Steve HELP! HELP! Lonna took off walking a little slowly keeping her eye on the squirrel, and the squirrel had its eyes on her! Steve was pretty close, so it did not take him long to run over to help Lonna. He did not know what was going on until he got there. Right when he got there, the squirrel jumped up onto Steve's leg! It was trying to run up his leg! No one wants to get bit by a squirrel, because their teeth are so sharp and strong! A squirrel can bite into a Hard nut, so you know what they could do to your skin. He took the end of his gun and tried beating the squirrel off with the stock of his gun. The squirrel, fell back to the ground for a quick minute; Steve pulled out his pistol he was wearing on him, and shot the squirrel . He got it! Lonna and Steve were both shook up. All the screaming and hollering Lonna did, scared off all the squirrels for a long way. So they just went back to the farm. They were done hunting for that day. Steve bought Lonna A safer gun! And nothing like this, ever happened again!! We told Jeff, and Grandparents what had happened, and they were glad we did not get hurt! We wish we could have brought back some squirrel's, for Grandma can make some of the best tasting Fried squirrel, milk gravy and biscuits you ever ate! There will be another day real soon we told Grandma; and every one else. We also hunt for rabbit, deer. It is food on the table and good for you too! We hunt because it is fun, and it puts food on the table. We have an orchard full of fruit trees and black berries. When we first bought this Farm, it was all growed up with honey suckle, weeds, thorn trees it was in a terrible mess. It took a lot of work to get it, as nice as it is now! We had help from our son Jeff. Our niece, and two nephews. Plus Steve and Lonna. It was too hard of work to clear everything for Grandparents to help. So we got started on the worst looking place. We all had the tools we needed to do this work. We worked for almost four hours, then finally one of the nephews said; hey look what I found. By golly, there it was our great big barn. We found one side door, that was cleared off first.

Because that is where we all started working in that area. We finally got to where we could open the door. And walked inside. It was amazing! We had a barn that we did not know was even there. This barn was forty by fifty foot! It was nice inside. Needed a few boards replaced here and there. But it was so nice to find, in the middle of all that mess growing all around it. I mean you could not tell there was a barn there at all! So this was our first project. We were so happy to find this, we just kept right on clearing the weeds away. Until a week or so went by. Then we had us a nice looking barn that you could actually see, inside and out. We were all proud of our hard work we did. Now there was one more bad spot to clear. Hopefully we would find something in that mess too! Well we had been working on that spot for a few hours, when Lonna let out a loud horrible scream! She had a machete, in her hands. That is what she was using to clear away the weeds and honey suckles with. This brownish grayish, blackish thing came straight up off the ground, about three to four feet; Lonna looked at it, thought it was a big bug. Then it opened up its wings! It was a great big BAT!! It looked straight into her eyes, and flew straight towards her like it wanted to kill her! She was screaming HELP HELP! She was so scared she threw down the machete, and took off running as fast as she could! Steve came running over there to see what was wrong! Lonna told him. Steve said he saw something chasing her. And yes it looked like a bat! It was a Bat. He asked Lonna, why did you through down your machete? You could have used that to protect your self! She just told him, she was so scared, she just wanted to run and get away from it! Before it was to bite her! They are ugly, and they do carry rabies! Any way Lonna did no more clearing for a few hours. Not until she calmed down. Then she worked in another area. Steve thinks the bat must have been sleeping or sitting on a nest. He finished that area! Plus, there were lots of snakes out there in all that grown up thick mess of growth. Finally, they realized; there is an orchard in there! So they carefully kept up the hard work, until the orchard was all cleaned up, and looked so pretty. Then, they learned how to take care of the fruit trees. There was apple trees, plum trees, pear trees, peach, cherry trees, and lots of Black berry bushes. We get to eat lots of pies. And also make lots of really good jelly. The black berry's made the best jelly! And very good black berry cobbler. These black berry bushes had stickers on them. So we were always getting stickers in our fingers and arms. But it was sure worth it! Some of the black berry bushes are in the cow fields too. The cows loved them. The stickers did not seem to bother them.

The horses did not like them. But the horses loved us to give them any of the apples or the pears, that we would give them. Not too many at one time, or they may get a belly ache. We do not spray our fruit trees with no chemicals. So this was called, the organic way of growing them. Which is best for us, no chemicals! Now that we have the orchard all cleaned up, it is not hard to keep it that way. All that fruit is nice to have. Grandma sure keeps us in lots of good eating desserts!

We have a pond too. But it needed more Fish in it so we stocked it with 300 channel cat fish. And some blue gill, bass, croppie. Now they have all grown bigger, and they are lots of fun to catch and eat! Sometimes our neighbors will come over to help us catch enough for a big fish fry. It is a fun way to spend time with our neighbors and family, friends. One time there was a big muskrat in our pond. They are not good to have in a pond because they will dig holes in the sides of it. And this will cause the water to leak out. They can literally tear up the walls of a pond. One day our dog was swimming in the pond, when he saw this BIG Muskrat. Joe Joe went after it! The fight was on! They fought for a long time in the water. The whole time, which means old Muskrat would bite Joe Joe right in his face, then the dog would bite him back! Sometimes they would go under the water and you could not see either one of them! This went on for at least twenty five minutes. Finally Joe Joe won! He was bleeding on his face and nose, from all the muskrat bites. We doctored him up. And he was just fine. Grandma took a rake and picked up the muskrat with it. The muskrat was very heavy. She put it in the back of Steve's pickup truck. To keep Joe Joe from trying to keep biting on it. We wanted Steve to see it when he got home from work. Steve heard all about what had happened. And he sure was proud of Joe Joe! We never had any muskrat troubles again! In the evening we feed the fish. We buy our fish their food from the feed store. Helps them to grow very big. Some of the fish weigh up to ten pounds. There are also turtles in the pond too. Once in awhile we do see a snake. We just stay away from them. They eat a lot of things like mice, and other little varmints. Bad thing is they also eat bull frogs, or any kind of frog. They are no trouble to us if we leave them alone. There is a type of snake, called a King snake. They like to try and eat things like baby ducks, or even our little chicks. Grandma saw a snake in the little houses, where the chickens lay their eggs. By the time she found it, the King snake had already swallowed four to five eggs, whole. You could see the round shape from the eggs in its belly.

Swallowing the eggs made the snake so fat it could not get back out of the little holes in the chicken's fence. This means they are trapped inside the chicken's cage. These snakes are very mean to animals, people, or dogs too. So Grandma said we have to get rid of this snake. Once they find the eggs, you can never keep them from coming back for more. They can get very big. This one was about five feet long! There are bull frogs in the pond too. We love to listen to them make their croaking sound that they make. They eat a lot of bugs. We enjoy the frogs in the pond. Some people go out frog gigging. But we do not allow this in our pond. If we want to go, we frog gig at the back of the Lake. You gig for frogs at night. Which means it is going to be dark out. A gig is a long pole, with forked sharp points on the end of it. It is not easy gigging for frogs. It takes one person to hold the flash light so you can see them. And one or two people to do the gigging. There are hundreds of mosquitoes always biting at you. This part is the bad part. Also there are a lot of snakes in the trees and bushes. Some times the snakes get in your boat. We usually use a canoe. You just get them out with a paddle. When you do gig a frog, we put them in a burlap sack, or a cooler will work too. Once you get enough to fry up, it is time to go home. Thank goodness, because the mosquitoes have almost drained you dry of your blood. Well not really, it just feels that way. Once back at the farm the men will get them already for cooking the next day. Bull Frogs are Very tasty! Lonna and Grandma fry them up, and boy do they taste so good! Lonna really loves them. We all love them.

Also on the pond is about four or five Ducks. They lay their eggs close to the pond. And the mom and dad, keep a close eye on them. So, as nothing will try and eat them. When they hatch they get in the water and follow their parents around. They are so cute! Come fall they will fly south where the weather is warmer. But every spring they will fly back this way, and land on our pond. This makes us very happy! The ducks like to be left alone so we just watch them. The ducks will eat any left over fish food that floats their way, after we feed the fish. We usually have a camp fire burning while we fish. That way if you get tired of fishing you can sit by the fire and visit with the other people who are there. It is warm and relaxing. When it is time to feed the fish we like to watch them eat. They come to the top to eat. Because the food we feed them floats. You can see their big mouths open up to scoop up all the food they can. Feeding them makes them healthy, and they love it.

When it comes to the Garden, we know this is gonna be FUN! And we will all get together to work on planting the vegetables. We also like to plant some flowers. Especially Giant Sun Flowers!! They get so big and are very pretty. After the garden is planted, there are still things to do in the garden. Like make sure they get enough water. And keep the weeds out. This helps to keep the bugs out. Plus it gives the plants more sun light. Grandma and Grandpa sure do know a lot about gardening. They teach us all kinds of interesting things. They have had many years experience. So we listen to them, and learn so much. We grow a lot of different things in our Garden. Tomatoes, lettuce, spinach, green onions, radishes, broccoli, cauliflower, potatoes, Bird house gourds. You can make bird house gourds into decorations. Or make them into bird houses. Usually wren birds like to make nest in them. Also we grow watermelons, cantaloupe, sweat corn, peppers. Lots of different kinds of peppers to grow. We like to plant zucchini. It is really good to fry up with a fish fry. Be careful when picking your zucchini. Several different times Lonna would get ready to pick a zucchini and it would turn out to be a snake. When they are ready to pick a snake looks a lot like a zucchini. This has happened, and it will scare you. We also plant turnips. Grandma can cook them so good and tasty. Grandma and Grandpa are very good cooks. And we grow okra. This is so good fried. We plant green beans too. This is a favorite, to all. There are many ways to cook these vegetables. We grow carrots and beets too. Sometimes it is good to just wash them off and eat them fresh. Maybe in some kind of dip. We grow so much that we get to share with family, friends and neighbors. Our neighbors come over and visit us all the time! This is nice of them! Plus they appreciate all the eggs, and vegetables we give to them. And the good fish fry's. We appreciate all their help too. So having our Garden is fun and rewarding. We get to eat good healthy food from the Garden and share with others too. We love having the farm, and all the things we find to do on it. Every day is a new experience!

So having a farm is truly a lot of fun! Fun for us and so many other people, even the animals we raise. Even the chores are fun, when you are with the ones you love. We enjoy the Orchard, Garden, camp fires, fishing riding the horses, gathering the eggs. Specially, getting together with so many nice people. Really makes each day, FUN ON THE FARM!! And exciting. Never know what will happen next!! READY OR NOT!

The End for Today!

Printed in the United States
by Baker & Taylor Publisher Services